TO BE A WINNER

A book designed to motivate *you* to study and to reach your potential.

By Ian Newbegin (PhD)

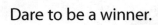
Dare to be a winner.

TO BE A WINNER

IAN NEWBEGIN

BALBOA.
PRESS

A DIVISION OF HAY HOUSE

Balboa Press books may be ordered through booksellers or by contacting:

Balboa Press
A Division of Hay House
1663 Liberty Drive
Bloomington, IN 47403
www.balboapress.com.au
1-(877) 407-4847

Because of the dynamic nature of the Internet, any web addresses or links contained in this book may have changed since publication and may no longer be valid. The views expressed in this work are solely those of the author and do not necessarily reflect the views of the publisher, and the publisher hereby disclaims any responsibility for them.

The author of this book does not dispense medical advice or prescribe the use of any technique as a form of treatment for physical, emotional, or medical problems without the advice of a physician, either directly or indirectly. The intent of the author is only to offer information of a general nature to help you in your quest for emotional and spiritual well-being. In the event you use any of the information in this book for yourself, which is your constitutional right, the author and the publisher assume no responsibility for your actions.

Printed in the United States of America

ISBN: 978-1-4525-0252-6 (sc)
ISBN: 978-1-4525-0251-9 (e)

Balboa Press rev. date: 08/27/2011

For my Grand children, Joshua, Zachary, Hannah, Grace, Jamie, Robert, Mika, Hayley and Riki. May they enjoy success in their lives.

———————————————

Nobody makes a greater mistake than he who spends his life trying to avoid them. (Anon)

———————————————

Preface

This book contains thoughts and ideas about *self improvement* and popular quotes and stories that relate to the development of *you,* a student seeking success. The quotes and stories are not mine. I collected them throughout my years of teaching and apologize to the authors if I misquoted.

I believe that *every* student has the potential to achieve greatness. I will not single out anyone and I expect you to do the same. *Everyone* can be successful; it only requires them to believe it and take action. Yes, it may take a lot of work, but if you are up to it, why not be the best person you can possibly be?

Success as a student requires **work**, *not ability*. **Effort** is the key element for achievement. It is easy to say that anyone can fail; just don't do the work, but, it is just as easy to say that anyone can pass, and pass with good grades. All it requires is effort and a <u>belief</u> that *'I can do it.'*

*Every day in every way, **YOU** are worth the effort.*

There's a saying, 'nothings either good or bad but thinking makes it so.' Whenever you say 'Hell, I don't want to do this, it's boring. I hate it!' Your thoughts have made this statement true, at least, true for you. But when you look at it, there is nothing really wrong with studying, or doing homework. They are actions which are either done or not; *of themselves they are neither good nor bad.* However, when *you personalise* it, then it becomes bad because *you own* it. This book will show you that you can achieve what may seem impossible. Yes, you can do it.

Maximize your chance for success at school by engaging in work practices that will improve your future outlook and study ability. Remember one thing while you read this book; the effort **is** worth it. YOU are worth it. Give yourself a real chance.

Table of Contents

IF.......

- If you are comfortable with the way you are progressing at school and don't plan to do anything different in the future, then stop reading now. Don't waste your time.

- If you believe that by reading this book, you will probably not do anything different to improve your education, then stop reading now.

- What! You're still reading? Could it mean that you want to improve your grades? Could it mean that you want to improve your chances in the future? Hey! If that's the case; read on.

- **You** can improve your grades in **any** subject. You can be the best *'you'* possible by working to improve yourself. It requires effort, are you up to it?

- If you are willing to put in the effort, if you are willing to try a little harder, if you are sincere about being the best person you can possibly be, then by practicing the simple ideas suggested in this book, <u>you will succeed</u>.

- Work hard, try your hardest and never give in. YOU are worth the effort.

- Oh, I need to tell you that there a lots of questions asked in this book. Take time to answer them for yourself. You don't need to write the answers, just be honest and answer then in your mind.

Learning cycle.

Hey, you've reached the first section! It's about learning and you know what? We all learn in different ways. Some of us are visual, others more auditory and yet others are kinesthetic, or put another way; 'touchy feely'. We are generally more of one than any of the others, but, we have a bit of all three learning styles in all of us.

We might learn in different ways and even find learning difficult, but learning is cyclic (or goes round in a circle).

There are many degrees of learning. Some students seem to learn within one particular subject area, better than they do in other subjects.

A simple learning cycle for *all types* of learners is provided below. Given that learning is cyclic, if you miss any part of the cycle, then there will be a strong likelihood that you will get lower grades than anticipated. *Success requires work.*

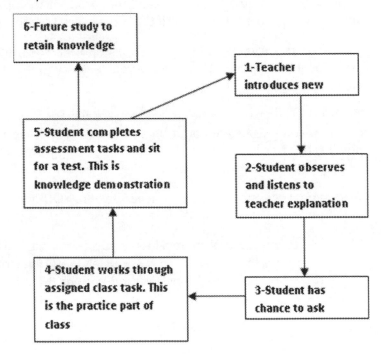

I told you that learning, and your future success, requires work. Are you still willing to read on? Take a closer look at the learning cycle.

Don't you already do this in class?

Maybe you are guilty of missing one of these elements, (I bet it's stages 2 and 3) and as a consequence to this, you miss *the* point of a particular lesson.

Active attention to the lesson being presented does not mean talking with another student. If you miss the point of the lesson, you are also less likely to ask questions. Even this aspect of learning is cyclic. Once you miss a key element of a lesson, your behavior will be such that you will miss the entire concept. You will go from non learning to non learning and as your circle increases, *you will continue to not learn*. Is it worth it?

Personal discipline is important for learning. Once you have mastered the art of *attending to the lesson*, you will see improvement. In time, you will see that each lesson flows into the next and might even depend on what you have learnt at an earlier time. Ah yeah, last year's work *is* important. What you learn *during* the year should be *retained for the future*. It doesn't mean you have to study over the long holiday break, it means that you *need to attend to the work when it is presented*.

Ah well, this is what learning's about. Connecting ideas and building a bigger picture. We have to know the basics before we can expand on a subject. It's that simple. Be present and engaged, and learning will take place.

Think of a time in class when you was 'off task'. How were your grades when you were tested on the concept presented by your teacher? Could they have been better?

Keep reading. There's a lot of good stuff to come and, it's all about you.

Student performance measures.

What on earth are student performance measures? Do you need to know about these? Think about it. How are you going to maximise learning, if you don't know about your performance? How well does an elite athlete or dancer know their performance?

"Oh! I haven't done any homework all year. Ah well, if I pass it will be a bonus," is this attitude how we pass?

The following questions have been designed to help you determine whether or not you are working to the best of your ability in *"every"* subject. A 'yes' answer suggests adequacy in that particular area. A 'no' answer suggests that you should *address the reasons* for answering 'no' to a question so that you can improve your work and study ability.

Consider your best and worst subjects. Ask the following questions of yourself:

Did I *understand* the lesson in each subject?

Do I *ask questions* in class to help me to understand the work?

Have I *completed* all set work?

Do I *complete the work set* in class?

Do I put in the *same effort* for my best and worst subjects?

Do I *allow time* at home to *complete* the work in both subjects?

Have I *planned the use of my time* to enable me to study and complete homework?

Am I *comfortable* with my current level of work in both subjects?

Do I develop a *plan of attack* to help me to solve a problem or complete a task?

Have I given myself the *best chance* to pass each subject?

Do I *listen to* the teachers instructions and *follow* those instructions?

Am I *easily distracted* by other students?

Is my current thinking about the subject, *positive?*

Can I change my *thinking* about my worst subject to improve my grades?

Remember: *If it is to be, it is up to me.* (Unknown)

Who said that two letter words strung together can't produce a profound statement!

If you answer 'no' to any question, take time to think about why you said no and how you can correct the performance in that area.

The level of *your* performance in any subject is dependent on the level of attention given to the subject material being presented.

Question: Can your teacher learn the material presented in class, for you?

Who determines your level of understanding?

I know that I determine my level of understanding, and I'll keep learning for as long as possible. What about yourself?

If you have taken on board what I have said so far, you are already on the path to success. If you are still keen about improving your grades, keep reading.

Pathways.

Do you *know* where you want to be in ten years time? Do you care?

Consider the following excerpt from Alice in Wonderland (*Lewis Carroll*, Disney movie version).

Alice: (at a fork in the road seeks direction) Please Mr cat, can you tell me which path I should take?

Cheshire cat: (sitting in a tree at the fork in the road). It depends on where you want to go?

Alice: Oh, I don't know really.

Cheshire cat: Then it doesn't matter which path you take.

The trouble with following 'any-old' career path without thought, or because of the *consequences* of poor study techniques, is that you may end up, unhappy. You may end up in a job which lacks security, promotion or even challenge.

See! There is a point to learning. **You** improve **your chances** for doing what you want when you leave school.

Know where you would like to go in life. Select the right path.

It is better to follow a career choice than to fall *into one. (unknown)*

Schools offer a variety of pathways, all of which lead to success. Schools *do not* offer pathways that leads to failure; *that is your choice to make*. But, would you deliberately make this choice? I have never worked in a school where students were offered a chance to follow a path that led towards failure.

Every teacher, every school, wants to pass the students. I didn't tell my students to fail; I did my best to help them gain a pass.

A student's *action* in class will dictate whether that student will pass or fail. It's that simple! Work, concentrate, make good choices, and passing *is* assured.

You have your life ahead of you. Make the right choices along the way and enjoy the rewards. As I have said before, y**ou** are worth the effort.

Honesty.

Believe it or not, success at school also depends on honesty. If you can't be honest *with yourself*, what's the point in going on? We *fool* ourselves when we *lie* about our behaviour. Yes, you might get away with it for a while, but what do you gain?

Answer the following questions for yourself, but be honest.

Do you *blame* others (your teacher perhaps) for your lack of understanding of a particular topic?

Do you *question* your own *behaviour* in class and assess it to be appropriate for leaning?

Do you make *excuses* for not completing the class work set?

Do you make a *conscious decision* to chatter with class mates during a lesson rather than listen to the lesson?

Do *you* complete your homework, or do you copy from someone else?

Is it more important for you to *socialise in class* than to do the work set?

Listen to your *'self-talk'* as you answer these questions. *Study your feelings*; how comfortable are you with your answers? If you experience discomfort when answering these questions, even if it is a feeling, work to improve your outlook. If you just skimmed through the material above, *take the time to answer the questions and explore your feelings*. Please, don't shrug it off, your feelings are real and your future behaviour depends on what you think about them, and what you plan to do about them.

How you manage your feelings in the future will affect how you make choices and enter the workforce. Doing nothing might alleviate a feeling, but, you will not achieve your best. Feelings play a big role in where we go in the future.

Be the best person you can possibly be.

What's the saying? *Honesty is the best policy*.

Why build an environment based on deceit? Be honest with yourself, you'll *feel* great! And you know what! You might even find a solution to your study problem.

The Blame Game

School life is no different to life outside of school. We are all responsible for our actions. Looking for *excuses* or *someone else to blame* for your failures will not help to improve your grades.

If you blame your teacher for poor grades, how will this help you to improve in the future? All you will be able to say is, 'See! I told you it was ..." and guess what! *You will continue to fail!* Take control of your actions.

Look at *yourself* for the root cause of any failure. There is a very high probability that *if you change your habits or behaviour towards a subject or teacher,* then, **you will succeed**.

Conquering others requires force. Conquering oneself requires strength. (Lao Tsu) **You** gain nothing by forcing the blame on to someone else. Conquer your *fears* and seek success.

How are you going with this stuff? Do you still believe what I have said? Are you still willing to achieve success by changing your learning behaviour?

Of course you are, that's why you are still reading. Keep going, you'll see that it's all worth it in the end, because, YOU will be successful.

Of Heaven and Hell.

In all things we do, some people make a Heaven of hell while others make a hell of Heaven. Do you turn a miserable activity into a positive experience, or do you complain about it? Do you enjoy a pleasant experience or do you make it into a 'horror' event? You know; you have a choice! How you *view* a situation will determine whether it will be Heaven or Hell.

Consider the following modified biblical story.

A group of people in Hell where gathered around the evening meal table which was amply supplied with excellent food. Everyone had an over sized knife and fork tied to their hands so, they couldn't get food easily to their mouth. This caused a lot of frustration and the people soon turned against one another, hurting, or killing their neighbour.

Meanwhile, in Heaven, the exact same meal and exact same conditions for its patron's occurred, but there was much laughter. The people fed each other with their long forks, thus, everyone had a hardy meal and fun at the same time while supporting their friends in Heaven.

What about you? Do you *fight* with kids in your class? Do you *work with* others in your class or against them?

When students in a class room are in harmony with each other, *learning progresses*. However, when students fight with each other and pick on a student because he/she is achieving, *learning is minimised*.

Work with your fellow students, not against them. You will enjoy your classes more, and the learning will be rewarding.

You could say we live in heaven right now. *It's up to you what you make of your life!* You don't have to die to be in heaven. You can be in heaven right now by adopting a positive attitude towards life and your education. You do not need to make a hell on earth because of poor choices.

The significant adults in your life are role models. Yes, they might sound like they are telling you what to do, but they mean well. Whether you follow their advice, or do what they say is up to you. It will be the devil in *you* that stops *you* from learning, not your significant others. No one tells you to stop learning, no one that is except, inadvertently, yourself.

If you are forever looking behind your back to see who is watching and you avoid doing homework, life can be hell. Think about it. If you take a positive approach towards learning, and life, you will feel a hell of a lot better. Pardon the pun.

Oh, by the way. Those of you in the class who want to learn would be doing the class clown a favour by telling him (or her, but I bet it's him) to be quiet. In fact, tell any kid who's disrupting the class to be quiet, after all, they are abusing your time.

Dream, and it might come true.

"Dream, and it might come true," are words out of a Roy Orbison song titled, 'Dream'. The word 'might' is very important since when we dream of success, it only *'might'* come true, depending on whether *'action'* is taken.

We all 'day dream' from time to time. Some dream of athletic success, while sitting on a seat. Someone else dreams about artistic success, while sitting on a seat. Yet again, someone else dreams about academic success, while sitting on a seat. What is the common element here? *'Sitting on a seat.'* If the dreamer doesn't get off his or her backside, then the dream is only a *'might come true'.*

Success occurs close to the level we dream, when **action** is taken. Dreaming alone only provides comfort, that's why so many people never achieve their dreams because they do not take action, they stay with their dream, they stay in their 'comfort zone' and will never know success as it can be. Yes it is true, dreams can make us feel good, so we dwell on the dream, harboring it; just so that we feel good.

"Only in dreams, in beautiful dreams," you guessed it, another Roy Orbison song, but if you stay only with your dreams, success will not be realized.

It is critical for any improvement or success that **action** takes place and that the action is directed towards your success or desired goal.

Time management

We each have *exactly* the same amount of time, 24 hours in every day. How we use it is entirely up to each of us.

Some students *use their time wisely*, others just do what happens to feel right at the moment. How do you use your time?

At school, you are *expected* to attend all classes. Do you? If not, this is an *inappropriate* use of time.

During class, you are *expected* to listen to instruction and to complete the tasks set. Do you?

At home, you are *expected* to study or catch up with the day's work. Do you.

At home, you are *expected* to complete certain graded tasks. Do you?

Do you have time to do the things asked above? If not, you need to manage your time better.

Do you have a study time-table that allows you to plan the use of your time?

Do you plan to have a sport or relaxation time, or do you just take the time?

Try *organising* the use of your time at home by using a *study time-table*. Build in sport or recreational time, you deserve it.

Studying by chance, or because it is the day before a test, usually results in low grades. Why continue this habit? Improve your success rate by *planning* your study time.

Your time-table could look something like this:

Time day	Monday	Tuesday	Wednesday	Thursday	Friday	Saturday	Sunday
4.30-5.00		Basketball training					
5.00-5.30							
5.30-6.00		Scan days work					
7.00-7.30		HW-English					
7.30-8.00		Other HW					

Fill in the times to *suit your needs*. List the activity in the blank spaces. **Keep homework and study separate**. One day is done as an example. Note that you will need to decide on the time line (Study time period), I set from 5.30-8.00, but it can vary. Choose times that suit you.

Get into the habit of *reading* the days school work when you get home, even if it is just to glance at the work. By doing this, you will get to know what you know and what you don't know and therefore be able to correct the problem.

Home work is not studying. Homework is work set by your teacher for practice and assessment.

Studying is what you decide to do in a subject to improve your understanding of that subject. *Not studying is what you decide when you want to leave passing up to chance.*

It makes sense doesn't it?

The fact that you have read this book up to this point suggests to me that you want to improve your chances (or level) of success at school. Organise your time. It will also help relieve the stress of wondering what you should be doing that night. Don't forget to include sport and relaxation in your planning. It is important that you continue to do what you enjoy. I only ask that you plan what you do after school to maximise your chance of success while maintaining enjoyment.

It has been said that a cluttered mind leads to a very busy and disorganised schedule. Unclutter your mind and organise your daily activities and it will serve you well into adulthood. Disorganisation is a root cause of procrastination and indecision. If there is no plan to complete anything, then, why make the decision to complete a task when the time catches up?

There is another form of time worth considering, it is 'psychological time' and it is this time which causes the most damage. Psychological time exists, *now*. So, whenever you say, I won't do it now, I'll do it later, *you are saying it at the very time you could have put in more effort. NOW.*

Clock time ticks away, and once past, it will never return. Future time hasn't occurred yet and this form of time is a deep cause of 'procrastination', since, many procrastinators put things off until the future. You can plan the use of clock time, but it needs vigilance to ensure that you use it wisely. So, why not perform the set task at the earliest possible time, which may even be: *Now*. You are reading this book, now, in five minutes time (future) you may still be reading this book and it will be, *now*. When every you displace time, you are always doing it, *now*, So please, use your study time as planned.

Never give up

Consider the following story.

Two frogs where happily playing 'leap frog', when they came across a butter churn. "What's that?" One frog asked the other. "I don't know, let's go have a look," the other replied.

They hopped around the butter churn till they came across a stool. They leapt onto the stool and then into the churn which was filled with milk. "This is a strange liquid," said one frog to the other. "It doesn't seem to be harming us, let's swim around for a while," the other replied.

The two frogs swam and swam until they began to tire. "Let's stop and rest," said one frog to the other. Yes let's, but there is nowhere to sit," the other replied.

They tried to climb the walls which were too steep and soon, the two frogs were getting very weary. "I can't take much more of this. I am losing my strength," said one frog to the other. "Hang on. Don't give up. Something will happen just wait and see," the other replied.

"It's no use. I can't do it. Save yourself." And the frog sank slowly to the bottom of the churn.

The remaining frog cried out for its friend. It swam faster and faster around the churn grieving for his friend, when he noticed that the strange liquid was getting thicker. Before long, he could walk on top of the liquid and found that he could easily hop out.

If only his friend had tried that little bit harder, he too would have succeeded.

What about yourself? Do you 'give up' on difficult tasks? Think of the frog, don't give up, *ask* and/or look for support. Your success *may* depend on it.

Stay positive about your prospects.

We all live in the same world but with our own sense of reality. Some make it heaven and others a hell. (Anon) Sound familiar?

What do you think about studying? What do you think about your individual subjects? Are they heaven or hell? You know, it's up to you, I have already discussed this.

Develop an 'I can do' policy and you will make heaven of a hellish situation. Never give up. If you allow yourself to think that you can't do the work, then you will not be able to do the work. It's the self fulfilling prophesy!

You don't drown by falling in the water, you drown by staying there.

It is our attitude at the beginning of a difficult undertaking which, more than everything else, will determine its successful outcome.

Success is not a matter of common sense since what is sensible for me may not be for you. Along with your parents, I can only suggest ways of improving your grades; you have to do the work. Don't give in to temptation (like playing games), do your best.

Look for an alternative. A solution almost always presents itself for those who seek it.

When you are stressed about learning, or studying, take time to relax. Take time to sit in a quiet place and think about nothing or, something that you enjoy. Remove the stressful feeling; *don't own it and certainly, don't give in to it.*

Procrastination.

Procrastination is the thief of time.

Do not worry about tomorrow, for tomorrow will worry about itself.

*The most important time is **now**. Use it wisely.*

When we tell ourselves that we'll complete a task tomorrow, it is more likely that it won't get done. I am sure you have heard of the saying, *'tomorrow never comes.'* Think about it, when do we ever reach, tomorrow? Never! But, when will we reach Tuesday, 15July? There is a difference!

When you set a deadline, or have an urge to put a task off till another time; *set the date.* Don't leave it to chance. Write down *both* the date and task. Don't commit it to memory. Tuesday, 15July will surely pass, but tomorrow? Better still, do it now.

Be definite about your task completion times. Don't leave it till the last minute.

What about exam study time? Don't procrastinate. Leave at least, *three clear days for study.* By doing this, you will have time to consult a teacher or friend about any difficulties you may encounter. The day before **is** too late.

You need time to consolidate new knowledge. *Know* that you *understand* a new idea by reading it over, or by attempting more problems. *Thinking* that you understand is not the same thing. *Think* about that! Leaving it to chance is not learning.

Consider your own study and work habits. Do *you* put off studying or completing a task?

Procrastination is sole destroying. Yes, you might feel great for a short time because you have gotten out of completing a task *that needed completing*, but, you end up feeling poorly later when it has to be done. You might even feel depressed; you would certainly have good reason to be. When a task is put off until another day, **you** are the one who puts it off. **You** find it easier each time you put off completing a task because there are no immediate consequences and more often than not, **you** can easily rationalize the reason, albeit, irrationally.

Start a set task early and set a completion time if you can't complete it. Again, if you leave the task completion to chance, chances are, it will never get done. Be proactive. Do the work and reap the rewards. Remember, you *reap what you sow*. Success is gained through success producing habits.

Procrastination **is** the thief of time. Once given a task, the clock is ticking and very soon, the deadline approaches, often, catching an individual unaware. There is no more time-unless you negotiate for extra time. Who are you fooling? *Plan the use of your time and you will achieve your goals.*

Think about this. What grade do you get if you do not submit a graded task? Now be honest, how do you feel about this?

If you are serious about not doing the work then I suppose you are not procrastinating. However, if you do put off what should be done and you are a serious contender for procrastinator of the year, then maybe you need to join the procrastinators club.

Think about it, by being in the procrastinators club, you will be in the company of people who, like you, can make up a zillion excuses for getting out of work. You will live up to the groups motto, "Don't worry, I'll do it tomorrow," knowing full well that it won't be done since tomorrow is a myth. It is you know! The only time that exists is *now* because the only time you can do the work is *now*. Look, this is an excuse for you to not do the work and to continue getting poor grades.

Truly, tomorrow will never come since the day after the deadline, you can say, "I'll do it tomorrow," if I ask, "Is it tomorrow yet?" You can say, "No. Wait twenty four hours." It's fantastic! You can wait twenty four hours and tomorrow is still in the future. See? You never have to worry about completing a task provided you say to the task giver, "I will have it completed tomorrow." What a great excuse.

But do you really want to be like this? Do you want to forever, trade your 'tomorrows' for a broken promise, simply because you don't want to complete a task? "I can't be bothered" is not an excuse. It leads to depressed thoughts and behavior, so take a positive stance and say no to the procrastinators club.

In the long term, depression is a real issue when it comes to procrastination. Why? Because you will have *developed a way of thinking* which will allow you to put off anything, even things you know that should be done. Your excuse making abilities will be enhanced and along with this new anomaly, you *may develop depression* which, in the long term, will make you feel worse.

Let me demonstrate how easy it is to 'think' your way out of completing a task by procrastinating. We have already looked at 'putting it off until tomorrow'. This is also called the 'manyana' principal. There is a second type called the 'conditional manyana' principal. Yep, you guessed it, you can think: "I'll put it off until tomorrow because I need to get some additional information (the condition)." But will you get the additional information? Hey, it's not tomorrow yet, and, the person I was going to ask was busy. See how easy it is!

Here's another. You think: "God, I always fail this subject. I know, I'll study later when I feel better (a condition)." Yes, fear of failure can lead to procrastination as can fear of success. Yes, you read it right! You may think: "Hell, just because I got a B in the last test, they'll expect me to get a B again or do better." So, what do you do? Put it off so that you don't gain the success you surely deserve.

Here's another; *anxiety*. "Boy, I get nervous when doing tests. It's three days till the test, I'll start studying *tomorrow*." What a great 'downer' procrastination is!

You are worth far more than joining a bunch of lazy excuse makers. **You can** do the work so why not give it a go. Now!

Indecision

This topic should be included in the topic, 'Procrastination', but is so important, that it is considered separately.

Many people who are indecisive have too many tasks to do at *the same time*. The decision to choose what to do becomes a chore and, more often than not, they choose to perform a task that is not high in priority. For example, a student has home work, an assignment and reading to catch up on. The home work and assignment are due tomorrow and a test on math is the day after. What do you choose? He is behind with reading the course novels and everything suddenly becomes overwhelming. What does he do? Calls a friend. Let's face it, speaking to a friend is far easier and *feels* better than completing the set work, besides, he couldn't decide on which task should be done.

Lack of confidence can cause indecision and coupled with poor organization; imagine how difficult it may be to decide on what should be done.

How can indecision be overcome? *Use a diary* and set priorities for all of the work you need to complete. As the due date approaches, it is reasonable to assume that what was a priority five, one week ago, may be priority one, or two, now. Ah, that word, 'now'. It is very significant when you consider that everything you do is done, *now*.

Setting priorities and dates makes it easy for you when the *now* comes. Unlike tomorrow, *now* is forever present. Don't make excuses, organize your time and set priorities so that you can do the work when it needs to be done.

I cannot emphasize this more. The only time you have to complete a task is now. Tomorrow never comes, the future hasn't happened yet and when it catches up, it is now. The past is gone and what you believe about yourself in the past does not need to be true, now.

*You can do anything with **enthusiasm**. Enthusiasm is at the bottom of all progress. With it, there is accomplishment. Without it there are only excuses.* (Henry Ford)

How successful was Henry Ford? Look at the size and success of the Ford motor industry.

If you approach your study with enthusiasm, there is a strong likelihood that you will succeed. Approach the same study with trepidation and chances are, it will be left till the last minute or not get done at all. Hey! We're back to procrastination.

Enthusiasm not only *improves* your chance of *success*, but also for gaining better than *good grades*. It could be argued that the set tasks only need to be done. It can also be argued that the tasks need to be done to the best of your ability, otherwise, *mediocrity* results. We should all strive to be the most successful person we can.

Enthusiasm breeds success. Be enthusiastic and reach for the sky. After all, *'Aim at the sun and you may not reach it; but your arrow will fly far higher than if you aimed at an object on a level with yourself.'* (Judy Hawkes).

When you are enthusiastic about something, you don't have time to be depressed.

Enthusiasm helps to create a happy environment. Enthusiasm creates confidence and confidence improves your enthusiasm.

When are you ever enthusiastic? NOW! The only time you can be enthusiastic is in the now, the present time, that's why being present or attending to a lesson is important since this is the only time that you can be enthusiastic. You can't plan enthusiasm, it can only happen *now*, when you are attending.

Compare enthusiasm with procrastination. When you procrastinate, how do you feel?

When you are enthusiastic about something, how do you feel?

Which is better?

Aim high. Shoot your arrow high and far. Give yourself a fighting chance for success.

Reach out for opportunities and perform the tasks with enthusiasm. It's contagious you know. If you decide to work hard and complete the work set, your friends will be influenced by this and, provided you are not distracted, they will soon follow you, particularly when they see how successful you are.

Never give up. Remember, **you** are worth it. Do you believe it yet?

But that was yesterday.

Stay in the day, tomorrow is a mystery, and yesterday is gone, and what happened, happened (Susan Thom). Do you dwell on all of your yesterdays? If you think you will fail a subject because history has shown that you always fail a particular subject, *then it is time to change the way you think.*

Yesterday and all that it represents *is gone*. It is history and *cannot be changed*. However, you can change your future. "No," do you say? What! You can't see yourself passing a subject that is pitched at your year level?

Your future is yet to happen. Everything happens in the *now*. What you do tomorrow and everyday thereafter will affect what you become. Do you know what you are going to do tomorrow? Have you thought about improving your chances in school? Success can happen- but, **you** have to be an *active participant*.

If you stay with your yesterdays, you may never improve. Change your thinking. Change your belief about yourself. *Give yourself permission to do better at school*, what happened in the past has gone and cannot be changed, ***but you can change your future***. After all, it hasn't happened yet! Your future will embrace all that you do. If you do nothing, then expect no change in your learning capacity. You are in control, at least; if you give yourself a chance.

Believe in yourself. Try different work habits in your 'pet hate' subject, and watch the results. **Think positively** about your future. Attempt all work. *Even small gains are a gain.*

Your mood state can be affected by dwelling on what has passed. Have you ever had something happen to you that affected what you did for days? Well, did you? Think about it for a moment. Did you share it with your friends? Did they sympathize with you? If they did, they have supported your mood, and you might go their again when things get you down.

Now, did what caused the thoughts, change? I have no doubt that you have changed what you thought about the event with time, but the event still happened and you decided to stay with it in the future (when the event occurred). You felt poorly- for no real reason. Change the way you think about things, including school work, and you should spend less time feeling low. Don't build on past events, build on your future.

Yesterday is but today's memory, tomorrow is today's dream. (Kahlil Gibran). It is OK to have memories of yesterday's successes and failures, but it is not OK to harbor deep feelings about yesterday, particularly if the feelings keep you dwelling on your mistakes and affect your progress. Yes, dream about tomorrow. Hold to the thoughts that you will do well, but take action. *Thoughts alone do not create a successful future.*

If today, *now*, you are sitting in class thinking about how much you hate the subject; if today, *now*, you are in class listening to idle gossip, if today, *now*, you are in class dwelling over something that upset you earlier; then you are abusing your time. These events will become part of your history and **cannot** change your future.

Go for it! Make what you want in life, happen. You **can** do it.

Walking the tight rope.

Have you ever been to the circus and watched someone walk the tight rope? Maybe you saw it on TV. Sometimes a net isn't used, so if the walker falls, you can bet that they wouldn't be walking on the ground for quite a while; that is if they survive. The walker takes his time. He places his foot carefully on the wire so that he can maintain his balance. *You can bet that he has practiced the walk many times*, each time, increasing the complexity of the walk across the tight, thin, wire rope by performing some stunts along the way. By the way, the walker could quite easily have been a female, so think about who ever you want in this picture. Why not yourself?

Studying can be likened to this activity. Ah, yes it can, don't scoff at my analogy.

When you began to learn, way back in grade prep (first year of school), or maybe, grade one, you were at first, uncertain. It was like walking the thin wire where you occasionally fell off, but being the little trouper that you were, as a little child new to school, you got up and tried again. Eventually, you succeeded.

Then we tend to get smart. Once we begin to learn, some of us 'widen' the wire. We use big planks instead so that the possibility of falling off is minimized. How do we widen the wire you ask? *By taking notice of what's going on in class.*

You know it's true! Look around your class; you will see some students still walking the thin, tight wire, falling off occasionally and getting back up to *try* again. Unfortunately, some students give up after years of failure, while others have developed a **habit** of studying, thereby **increasing** their chance of success.

But you have a thick plank! No way are you going to fall- unless the plank **breaks** because you become **complacent**, or want to *follow* others in the class by being *'cool'.*

It's not cool to be seen as being successful is it? I remember a student in year 8 who always got A's. He was smart and he knew it. His dad was proud of his efforts, and success came easily to him. I didn't teach him after year 8 and lost contact, until I saw him in the school yard one day.

"How's study going, Simon?" I asked.

"Ah, not too bad," he replied.

"Still getting A's," said I.

"Na, I'm averaging C's," Simon answered.

"Why? You were doing so well. What happened?" I asked in my best teacher, concerned way.

"I was getting picked on for getting A's and was being called a nerd, but I'll be OK," he replied confidently.

"I bet dads concerned," I suggested.

"Yeah, he's not too thrilled about it."

Simon was in year 11. I thought, *what a waste*, but when Simon completed year 12; *he topped the school!*

"What happened, Simon?" I asked excitedly.

"It was just an act. I used to study at home, and only produced C grade work for class. I didn't want to keep on getting poor grades."

What a clever Simon! Can you be so smart?

Apparently, Simon was **putting in the effort** and was always *walking the plank*, not the wire. In fact, Simon had built a bridge, making sure that he would not fall off. He faked his C grades, so that he could fit in. *But why should he have needed to do this?* Simon had ability, but the main contributing factor towards his success was the fact that he **put in and maintained the effort**. He knew he would get a good pass at year 12, because he had maintained the effort at home, albeit, quietly and secretively.

*You too can gain success. With effort and practice, **you** can succeed.* But don't hide it.

Don't walk the thin wire rope forever. Build bridges and make your future certain. Allow yourself to be successful and reward yourself however you like. You don't need to hide your success, be proud of what you do and never give up. The wire may be high, and so too can your goals. You can't climb the high wire and gain success without practice. When you do home work, you are practicing what you have learnt and working towards greater success. Think about it!

Give 110%

Our feelings and thoughts will determine what level of effort we will make to get us through the day. We don't think deeply about it, we just do it. The level we achieve is our 100% level for that day and what is 100% one day might be 80% or even 110% on another day.

So what am I asking here? You don't have to determine what level you will be achieving during the day, we do this automatically without any deep thought about it; what I am asking you to do is to give a **conscious** *10% more positive effort in everything you do during the day.*

Sound difficult? Well, no, it's really easy. Remember, you only need to think about what you are doing and whilst performing that action, give a conscious 10% more effort to improve or complete the task. *The 10% is determined on the day.* You make a *positive* decision *to do a little better* but when you consider it, 10% extra effort everyday will mean that your daily 100% level will improve along with your attitude to work. It will become the norm!

Think about it. If you give 110% effort towards everything you do, including your relationships, you can't lose. Develop a positive relationship with your teachers and notice how your reaction within the subject with that teacher changes. You will be the winner.

Think 110%. Make it part of your psyche and work will never become a chore.

Recapitulation.

Let's take time to look briefly at what has passed by thus far. Without looking at each section separately, what has been the key point about learning?

If there is anything that I want you to understand, it is the fact that **you** are the primary and major factor involved with **your** study and the grades you achieve. Let's face it, future success is up to you. Nobody can do the work *for* you. Nobody can get a job *for* you. Nobody can stop you from learning, *unless **you** allow them*.

If you agree with what I have said so far, then the main problem you might have to deal with is complacency. You see, it is very easy to see the big picture, but it is far harder to make it work for you, **particularly** if you have the habit of dismissing activities so readily. Most students should be able to organize themselves and stay motivated to improve their workability. It is the few who shrug off studying for other activities who need to think about their future and, if they have read this book, how they can change to improve their chances in life.

The following four sections are deliberately short since you will receive a heap of information from your teachers about how to study.

Make a summary

Make a summary of key ideas or key concepts for all your subjects. Use a high-lighter pen to mark important sections in both your work book and text book. *Use your highlighted points to generate your summary.* Listen to what your teacher suggests; any hint is worth noting.

Summarise in any fashion you choose. It's your summary.

If you are linear in thinking, *use dot points*. Mind-maps are another excellent way to summarise notes. Making a mind map encourages creativity and it gets you to think about the lay out.

How do you make a mind map?

- Start with a central idea with related ideas coming from it.

- Look for key points for each idea you create.

- If necessary, make new links. When you map ideas in this fashion, you create a logical path for understanding.

- Use colour and different shaped boxes for the ideas. The computer provides you with plenty of choices.

- Use different font sizes and **bold** key points.

- If the mind map gets too large, break it up in to a second map. Expand on an idea by making a map of that idea.

The mind map below, is of a simple model to help explain depression.

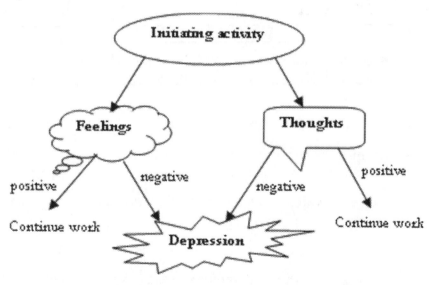

When you initiate an activity, such as procrastinating, you produce associated feelings and thoughts, usually negative. You may feel great for a short time, but as the time gets closer to submitting the work, you may feel anxious. In terms of thought, you might think *no problems, I'll start on it tomorrow* and when tomorrow catches up, you don't complete the task and you feel depressed. Ah, the irony of life.

When you study.

Studying is important for gaining good grades. You know this! That's what this book is all about. Well, I suppose it is also about how you can improve your chances of gaining good employment prospects, or getting great university entrance scores, but more often than not, being successful at school comes down to that magic word, 'study'.

When you study:

- Choose a quiet, *people free*, zone.

- *Enjoy* your study time.

- Sit at a desk or table with your study material *organised* around you.

- If you need music, *don't let it dominate*. Have it on low.

- Keep highlighters with you and *highlight important components of the work*. Highlight your work book and/or text book during the lesson.

- Read the highlighted material *regularly*.

- *Attempt* problems, even if they have been done earlier. Redo and/or read through problems.

- *Take a break* after about thirty minutes. Get a drink or something to eat.

- *Make a list* of questions you need to ask your teacher about.

- Study at least *three days* before an *exam*, longer for advanced subjects.

- *Plan your study time*. Study the hardest subjects earlier than the easiest.

- Don't leave anything to *chance*. Plan!

When you attempt an examination.

Examinations can be traumatic, but they are essential and an inevitable part of any course of study. No matter what year level you are in, the exam is important. It should not be ignored.

Before you attempt a test or exam, **relax**. Take time to *breathe* deeply to *calm* your nerves. You will perform better in the exam if you have a clear mind and the best way to get a clear mind is to take long, deep, breaths, both in and out.

When you attempt the exam:

- Take all relevant material to the exam, including working pens.

- Use the ten minute reading time to preview the questions.

- Attempt the easy questions first to free your mind for the hard stuff.

- Read the questions carefully and answer only what is asked.

- Don't spend too much time on a question, particularly low mark questions. If you are having difficulty, leave it and come back to it later.

- Be neat and organised. A messy page can create confusion.

- Don't guess answers. Use reason, you have seen the answer somewhere.

- At the completion of the exam, read it over. Check particularly, the questions you found hard.

When planning an assignment.

Assignments and essays require planning. They don't 'happen'.

Read the *requirements* carefully. Ask questions if you don't understand what is required of you.

Write down *key elements* of the essay or assignment.

Search relevant books and highlight key areas. Use page identifiers such as book marks.

Use the internet (if relevant) to search for the material for your assignment.

Once you have a good overview of what needs to be done, *jot down a plan* using headings and/or key concepts.

Use your plan to *write your first draft*. Be neat.

Read your draft, *make changes where relevant*. You may need to re-organise the information.

Write your final draft. Be neat, and don't forget to put your name on it.

Saying it as it is.

When you were born, you were given the same brain power as everyone else on the planet. So why are there so many bright people you may ask? The world is full of people who seem to have everything. They are smart, rich, and confident- they have it all.

The funny thing is, these people were born with no more brain power than you or me. One factor that may have influenced their success is their upbringing. Now I am not saying that your parents haven't done the right thing by you. Really successful people seem to develop an attitude which leads to success. They have successful parents and friends. They choose their friends carefully and form study groups which are supportive of their needs. But most of all, they are 'present' in the moment (*now*) and their constant presence and attention allows them to succeed.

Or, we could argue that life is unfair. It deals out the good and bad unrealistically, and you always seem to end up with a raw deal.

But! *We were all given the same brain power.* YOU are in control of your own destiny, the fact that certain things happen to you in your education, **is mainly due to you**. Whatever you do during the course of the day at school leads towards success or failure within a subject.

Why are you different? Is it because you have experienced failure earlier in life and believe that you will never do well in a particular subject? Alternatively, did you experience success, enjoyed the feeling and have been successful ever since? Either way, **you** created your pathway; **you** created the mind set, no one else.

You know what? I could sit back and say, "Look at all my fellow teachers. They are better than me. I'm just a mediocre math teacher," but I don't do this. If I did, guess what! I *would* be a mediocre math teacher. Why? Because I would have created the *mindset* that would ensure that I was mediocre.

Some students are comfortable with average grades, *as long as they pass*. "Mum and dad are happy as long as I do my best," I hear kids say. **But are they doing their best?** Are they trying to improve or is *near enough good enough*, "as long as mum and dad THINK that I am doing my best?"

Hey! Why not *do your best* and when you reach your best, **be better**. Sound silly? Then how else can we improve? Try it for yourself. Try to improve your grades in your weakest subject. If you are doing well in all subjects, try to do better. You will improve, you have choices and if you work at improving your grades, they will improve. **Remember; give 110%.**

Who told you that you cannot gain great marks? Is your brain any worse than that of any of your friends? Remember, you can gain success far beyond what you think possible.

If you are honest with yourself about improving your grades, then I encourage you to do something about it. All that I have said above still stands true. *Never* give up, use time management, *be enthusiastic* and so on but you need to know that you have always had it in you to improve your grades and to be the best student, adult, parent, worker-whatever, in the world.

If you are lethargic and well, *"I dunno. I'm different than others. I'm alright as I am,"* then do nothing but be warned; you will be doomed to never knowing what **you can** achieve in life.

How you feel *right now*, what you are thinking *right now* about your future, it is not set in concrete. *It is not real.* Your future hasn't been created yet, it is waiting for **you** to take action. Isn't it funny! We live in a dream about who we are and what we can be. We wait to see what happens rather than work towards achieving goals that we think are not meant for us. Who wrote the book of destiny?

Hey! *You are writing it right now.* Did you read that? NOW! We can only work in real time and in the *now*.

All of our futures are currently **unreal**. What I do *now* will effect what happens to me in the future. What you do from *now* on will affect what happens to you in the future. Do you want success? Then go for it. Never give up. Make it happen by learning everything you need to know about what it is you want to be.

I, and people like me, can provide tools to aid you in your attempt to gain success, but **you** are the only one who can achieve success for **you**.

You conscious mind tells you what you can achieve- if you believe it! *Your mind is not the truth,* it is your current perception of the truth, provided you don't query or challenge it. Our *subconscious* defines who we are. I am sure it doesn't have written, anywhere, that you are a loser, or that you will never be a huge success. It is *open to challenges*, but, your conscious mind often interferes. Tell it to butt out! If you want success, take the chance. Go for it. As I have said often throughout this book, *'you are worth the effort.'*

Whenever you feel 'down', whenever you have negative thoughts about doing school work, challenge your thinking, and analyse the feelings. If you do nothing, if you dwell on the negative, if you 'shrug off' the idea that you can improve both your grades and future prospect, then?

Success is yours if you want it and work towards achieving it. Don't give in. Set goals and work steadily towards being the person you want to be. Think positively and change your work habits after all, *you are worth the effort!*

Use your energy wisely.

Just to stay alive our body needs energy. If you lie in bed and do nothing at all, you would still need energy. Whatever we do after we get out of bed requires additional energy. We all eat; this is how we get our energy. Now I am not going to give a talk about what to eat, but eating correctly ensures that we have sufficient energy to get us through the day, with energy to spare.

So what has this got to do with learning?

In the previous section, I said that what you *think* about yourself is likely what you will be. There's an old saying, *"I think, therefore I* am." Of course! We let our conscious memory dictate our actions which determine *who we think we are.* Your thoughts will dictate how you react towards studying, or even to paying attention in class. Whatever you do as a consequence of these thoughts will result in the use of energy. Even thinking requires energy. So, if you turn and speak to another student, then your energy is directed towards that student. You could say that the student *'robs'* you of your energy.

If you attend to the work set by your teacher, energy is used but, which is a better use of energy? Isn't the energy spent talking *unnecessarily* to another student, *a mis-use of energy*? You may go home, completely exhausted, but was it the learning that made you feel tried, or the talking? Mum might say, "Poor Freddy, he works so hard at school that he comes home tired." *But is this true?*

Consider for a moment that you are working in class and you get upset because you don't understand the work. How do you feel? If you throw a tantrum or stop doing the work, then you are misdirecting the use of your energy. If you blame others for your lack of understanding, you misdirect the energy. *Why not channel it into asking for support*, or slowing your work rate down, taking your time to learn how to do the task successfully. It makes sense doesn't it?

You are responsible for **everything** you do. You might follow others, but **you** make the choice. Why not choose success? Your parents might say, "Go and study," and you go into your room and play the computer. **You** made the decision; even if you had studied, **you** made the decision and your parents only *directed* you towards the task of studying.

I am certain you have understood what I have been saying throughout this book. *You are responsible for your learning* and you can achieve success.

Don't give in to your negative self-thoughts, they are not true. It is easy to talk yourself out of completing a task, *because you don't want to do it!* Your mind will provide you with a huge variety of excuses for not studying. Don't let it! You are in control of your mind, don't let it dictate the conditions. **Success requires energy and so does 'slacking off.'**

Imagine this. *"I don't get this stuff. I wonder if Jackie knows where Tim's going tonight?"* What's likely to happen? Will this student grasp what the teacher is saying, or will he turn to Jackie and talk. It takes energy and courage to over-ride your thoughts, particularly when talking seems far better than listening to an instruction. But when will you, or this student, listen? When will Jackie decide that she wants to learn something, not waste time with idle chatter? Are you going to be under the control of another student's whim just because they can't be bothered?

If you truly want success, *there is no room for complacency*. There is nothing wrong with attending to the work set in class. Don't be the class clown. Don't give into other student's wishes to talk. Put pen to paper and pay attention. Direct your *energy* towards learning, **you are worth** it. In the end, if you put in a greater effort to achieve success, this new level of effort becomes the norm, and you become more confident and successful.

Use your energy; wisely.

Ah, but my teacher...

Hey! Here's a strange thing. I am going to agree with you from the start of this section, that teachers can sometimes be the problem. Teachers can whine and complain that the class isn't working, yet, here you are trying your best. Teachers can sit in their seat at the front and never move, never ask questions *yet you need help*. Teachers can talk to the board, not the class and when they're finished, you are directed to the text to answer questions, *but you didn't get it*.

Your teacher might stand in front of the class with their arms folded and their eyes are saying, *'well, get on with it.'* Your teacher might set the same work for everybody, but you don't get it yet and here you are, having to try to complete the work, *unaided*.

This can be a real problem, but can you change it? Yes you can!

Have you talked to a coordinator, or counselor, about the difficulty you are having with a teacher? Speak up about the problem, don't endure it, but report only the truth. If, in the end, nothing changes, then change your mind set. *The teacher doesn't seem to care about me, so, I'll do extra work myself. I can always ask for help from someone else.* Why not ask a friend if they understand the work? Get support from whoever you can. Remember, *you are worth it*.

Above all things....................

My main contention with this book is to motivate you to consider your future seriously, through the mechanism of study. The process that I hope you will follow will be rational, based on careful consideration of your future. Remember, you are at school for a short time compared to your working life.

But it is up to you! How you think is out of anyone's control, barring of course your own thinking. A further aim of this book is to encourage *positive* self dialogue and encourage you to act in the present moment, rather than 'put it off'.

What I would like you to do right now is to stop reading and take a serious look at your life. Do you delay completing work? Are you walking the thin tight rope? Do you let others control your time, and consequently, control you? Are you self motivated? Do you drop what you are doing to entertain or be entertained by friends, even though you know the work is important?

Unless you take control, real control, with your life, *now*, then you may face problems in the future. Of course you may face problems if you are the greatest student alive, but you will be better equipped to handle them.

I won't conjecture about the world's future, you've heard it hundreds of times, what I want from you is a *serious commitment* to **think** about your studying and your future. Nobody can create success for you, success is of itself, a reward that must be earned and when you earn this reward, you will feel *empowered*.

So when does all this happen? **Now!** The only time you have to do anything is now, so why not take stock of your thoughts and actions and put them into practice, *now*.

In Monty Pythons Life of Brian, at the end of the film they sing, 'Always look at the bright side of life.' Life will always throw you a curve ball. What you do with it will determine the outcome and level of success achieved.

Go for it, you're worth it.

I suppose...

I suppose you could argue that what I have presented requires a lot of work.

I suppose that I might agree with you, but then I would ask, *'is it worth the effort?'*

I suppose you could answer 'yeah'. but...

I suppose I would say, 'it's up to you.' *It always has been up to you.* It's your strength of character that will determine whether or not you will attempt to work harder. BUT, you need to realise that once you are in the *habit* of studying, listening and doing, **it will cease to be extra work**. It will not be anywhere near as much work as you might imagine. In fact, you might even take on extra responsibility when you see that *the effort is worth it.*

You have the ability to succeed. **Believe it! You** can do the extra work and still have plenty of time to do the things you love. Aren't you worth the effort?

Study is like...

Have you ever compared studying to other activities? I am going to compare it to the practice of Karate, they are similar in many ways.

Just like school, to progress in karate you have to pass a series of gradings, the level of your progression being marked by the color of belt you wear. If you don't pass a grading, you stay on your current level until there is improvement to warrant giving the karateka (student of karate) the next level.

At school, you get a series of tests, assignments and homework which, if they amount to a certain level, you gain a pass in that subject. What is different from karate is that, at school, you are matched in age with your fellow students where as in karate, the class can be mixed, ranging in age from six to sixty.

In karate, students have to fight, perform set patterns (kata) and practice techniques. These form part of their grading which as I have said, if they pass, they gain the next level as signified by a colored belt. Imagine, a fifteen year old can be a higher rank than a fifty year old. It's all about achievement and wanting to perform at ones best. The ultimate goal for a karateka is to get their black belt and for most, to progress from there to a higher Dan level.

Shouldn't this be the same at school? Shouldn't a student perform his/her best to gain the most from their education? A karateka 'fights' to earn their rank and respect. Shouldn't a student 'fight' to gain the best possible grade and earn the respect of their peers?

A karateka is encouraged to practice and to perform their moves to the best of their ability, while trying to 'perfect' a technique. What about at school. Should students try to perfect their understanding within a subject? Why should attending school be a stigma to ones learning? Think back to when you first started school. Wow! How far have you come whether or not you liked it. Why not aim to do your best and complete your education with the best possible grades you can achieve.

I know you can do it, and I bet you know that you can too. Give it a go, you're worth it.

Final words.

Your education is very important. As you can see, it requires work to gain good grades, *but it is worth the effort.* You will feel great because of your effort but remember: it doesn't happen overnight.

Don't get despondent, or give up because you feel that your grades haven't improved as quickly as you would have liked. *They will improve.* Maintain the effort and above all, maintain your humour. Be positive about your future and you will succeed.

You are not bound by the things perceived, you are bound by the clinging (Tilopa). If you hold to the idea that you are 'no good' at a certain subject, then you will be creating a pathway towards failure. Don't cling to the past. Look to the future.

The turtle only makes progress when its neck is stuck out. (Rollo May)

Think about it! If you don't try to improve, then your progress will be very slow. Take risks, study to reach your full potential.

The time to repair the roof is when the sun is shining. (John F Kennedy)

Plan for the future for if it is left untended, you may not have time to do what you want, when you want to do it. A good idea will only come to fruition if you plan when each action will take place. Any person or organisation can have success through innovation and careful planning, if you take the 'sit and wait' attitude; it may never happen.

We all have wisdom. I encourage you to take time out to be by yourself. Don't remain stuck in your thinking by listening to what friends say. Sit in a comfortable chair and relax. If you have practiced meditation, meditate. Wisdom is hidden deep within you. We all have the answers to our problems if we take the time to search *within* ourselves. Don't fall into negative self talk, tell your subconscious mind, or thinking mind to shut up. Challenge your thoughts, **find** a solution to your study or academic problems. You can do it if you try, believe me, you are not silly, so, relax and search within, let the wisdom feed your mind.

Good luck with your studies, you deserve success. Don't forget, *he who hesitates is lost.* Success comes with doing, not by waiting.

One sick joke before I pass over to you. Never by a Taits compass. Why? Because of what I said above; 'he who has a Taits is lost.' Think about it.

Good luck with your studies and continue to grow your life with love and success.

The Pung bird.

The Chinese are famous for their philosophy on life. They, like the Japanese, told many stories which had a moral, much like Aesop did with his famous fables. Read the story of the Pung bird and think about what the story is saying. *Never give up.*

The pung bird was a huge bird that lived in a tiny island with other birds. It was happy enough. There were plenty of other birds to play with and there was ample food and shelter. The other birds were a lot smaller than the pung which had a wing span of 500m. They used to laugh at its awkwardness, but he never let it show.

The pung bird used to speak about another land; one with lots of colour and variety, but the other birds used to laugh at him. The hawk was his closest friend and used to tell him about 'thermals' which occurred in the sky and how they could be used to glide effortlessly in the air.

The pung reasoned that if he flew high enough, he could use the thermals to glide to the other land that was hundreds of kilometres away. The other birds scoffed at the idea to soar high into the sky and glide to another land. "Stay and play with us. We have fun and don't have any enemies to worry us. Why do you want to do such foolish things?" they used to say.

One day, the mighty pung said goodbye to the other birds and took off for the distant land. He was ungainly and had difficulty getting into the air, the other birds look on in amusement as he seemed to have to run for miles to launch himself into the air.

Once airborne, he began his long climb. He used enormous amounts of energy to gain the height he reasoned would be necessary to achieve his goal. The other birds talked about the effort for many days and reckoned that it would take the pung one year to reach the height required for the journey.

At last the pung reached the height needed to take him on his journey. The pung was exhausted, but contented. He spread his huge wings and began to glide the long distance to the new land. One year later, he reached the new land and it was everything he thought it would be. It had plenty of food with an enormous variety to choose from. The trees were very large and plentiful and there was a great variety of other birds, full of colour. He was pleased. He had reached his goal. He reflected on his friends back home and remembered how drab their life really was. "They will never know what is here," he thought, then went quietly around exploring his new home of plenty.

Quotes and stories

Quotes and stories have been used to motivate people for many years. Aesop created many fables that are just as popular today as when he wrote them 2500 years ago. And what about Confucius? Around about the same time as Aesop, he developed a philosophy of life which is still quoted today.

You can pick up any newspaper, at any time, and find a quote that will motivate you, or read a quotation designed to motivate the populous. There are even famous quotes in movies! Remember 'Come up and see me sometime,' or 'Play it again Sam.' Not too motivating, but never the less, memorable; at least for us oldies.

Teachers often tell stories in primary, or elementary school to make a point. Do you remember listening to teacher tell the class a story?

This section is a compilation of quotes and stories that I have used at secondary (high) school. My students loved to hear them and if I forgot to tell them their weekly quote or story, they would remind me, or keep me to two quotes the next week.

Stories or quotes can have a different meaning for different people. I would read a quote to the class and ask the students for *their* interpretation. I always got a variety of responses. And who is to say that their interpretation is incorrect? I never corrected them; if the interpretation fits, let them own it.

I have also taken the liberty to offer a brief explanation of the quote or story, but, if you see another interpretation and it suits your needs, use it.

The Frogs in a well.

Two frogs lived in an old well that had little water for them to swim in, and a rocky outcrop on which they could live out of the water. When they looked up, they could see the sky. By day they saw a blue sky and occasionally, a grey, clouded sky. Rain would often fall into their well thus keeping their small pool with water. At night when they looked up they would see stars and occasionally the moon. At times, a bird would fly over the well but at no time did any animal stop and look into the well.

This was their life. They knew no other and their entire world consisted of what was visible to them from the well.

One day, another frog happened to jump onto the rocky edge at the opening of the well and looked down. "Come on down and take a look at our world," the two frogs called. "Why don't you come up and look at mine. There are trees and insects aplenty. You can swim in the huge lake and take comfort amongst the reeds." The other frog called back.

The older and more mature of the two frogs doubted what he had heard. He had never seen a lake nor heard of a tree and suggested to his friend that the frog above was lying and was working for someone else who wanted to kill them.

"No thank you." They called back and remained in the well for the rest of their days.

Look at the bigger picture and take risks. There is more to learn than what may be seen at the surface.

One giant leap.

A tadpole that had grown into a young frog was swimming around in a pond. He saw other frogs sitting on top of a rock and he watched them suspiciously.

"Come and join us," a frog called out.

"No thank you, it isn't natural for frogs to be out of the water," the young frog replied.

An older frog heard his comment and said, "No, you are wrong. When you grow into a frog you are allowed to get out of the water, but you must stay close to the water."

"No. I don't believe you. The other frogs have set up a trap for me."

The older frog shrugged, and swam over to a log and climbed on top.

Seeing that the older frog didn't join the others, the young frog swam over to the log and said, "I'm scared to get out of the water. What if I don't get to the top of the log?"

"If you trust me I will help you. Get your back legs onto the log and take a big leap. You won't fall. I will move to the side to give you more room."

The young frog did what he was told and leapt on top of the log. "This is great. I can see a lot more from here."

(Dare to take a risk, the results may be enlightening. Trust)

The monastery.

A long time ago when walking was a major form of transport between destinations, there existed a monastery that lie off a walking track, midway between two towns. Travellers often took this track rather than the road since it cut across a hill and shortened the distance. It also meant that there was less chance of getting run over by horses or carriages.

It usually took a day to walk the track to the neighbouring town. If however the traveller was stranded, they could seek refuge in the monastery for the night. The monastery however, was barely self sufficient so rather than turn travellers away, they issued a 'riddle' challenge, which if the traveller was successful in solving, would take the place of the monk issuing the challenge.

One day a traveller stopped and asked for refuge for the night. A young novice was sent to offer the challenge. The two men faced each other and said nothing for a while so the traveller thought that he may as well offer a riddle which was silent. He held up one finger to which, the novice held up two fingers. The traveller smiled as he held up three fingers which was countered by the novice holding up a fist.

The traveller conceded defeat but asked if he could speak to the Abbot before he continued his journey. "I must congratulate you on the quality of your monks. The young monk easily solved my riddle," he said to the confused Abbot.

"Tell me, what was your riddle?" The Abbot asked.

"I offered a silent riddle. I held up one finger signifying that there is only one God. He countered by holding up two fingers to signify God the father and his son. I held up three fingers in triumph to signify God the father, the son and Holy Spirit. But he saw through my riddle and raised his fist to say that God is all embracing" The traveller then took his leave and continued his journey.

The Abbot was still confused since had been having trouble with the novice. He called him in and asked what had happened.

"I don't know! I was thinking of a riddle when the traveller looked at me and held up one finger to say that I had only one ear. I thought that I would be polite showed two fingers to say that he had two ears after which he became rude and raised three fingers to say yes, we have three ears between us." He raised his fist to the Abbot as he said, "this made me so angry…."

What others think about you. Self image or self consciousness.

Stone Mason.

A Stone Mason was chipping away at the base of a cliff when a prince passed by. The Stone Mason thought "The prince is more powerful than I am, I would love to be a prince."

A genie replied "and so you shall," WOOSH, and the Stone mason became a prince. He ordered new towns to be built and was savage towards his followers. One day, he was driving a chariot when he felt hot and faint. He thought, "The sun is more powerful than I am, I would like to be the sun." The genie replied, "and so you shall," WOOSH and the prince became the sun.

He enjoyed the power where he could dry up rivers and destroy crops when one day, a rain cloud blocked the sun's rays and prevented him from destroying more crops. Ah, that cloud is more powerful than I am, I would like to be the cloud." Again the genie replied, "and so you shall," WOOSH and the sun became a big rain cloud.

The cloud rained all over the land causing great floods. He was happy until a wind came along and blew the cloud out to the sea where it could do no damage. "Wow. The wind is more powerful than I am, I would like to be the wind." "And so you shall" said the genie, WOOSH and the cloud became the wind.

He enjoyed this new power. He caused huge waves on the sea turning shipping vessels over and blew the top soil away so that farmers could not sow their seed. He destroyed buildings and made life quite difficult for the people then one day he came upon a cliff. He blew and blew but could not move the cliff. "The cliff is more powerful than I am, I would like to be the cliff." As usual the genie replied, "And so you shall," WOOSH and the wind became the cliff.

The cliff stood proud and tall, overlooking all of the land. Neither the sun, rain or wind could move it. One day, the cliff heard a clinking sound. It was a Stone Mason chipping away at the base of the cliff. The cliff thought, "The Stone Mason is more powerful than I am, I would like to be the Stone Mason." "And so it shall be," said the genie, WOOSH and the cliff became a Stone Mason and lived happily ever after.

Wishing to be more than you can be; Be the best you can with your current situation.

The priest and the prostitute.

A priest had the habit of meditating under a big oak tree in front of the monastery. He was seen by the community as being a holy and good man. He never caused trouble and helped those in need. One day while meditating, he looked out onto the road and saw a prostitute standing outside of a building. A man came up to her and they entered the building together.

The priest thought about what the woman was doing and it discussed him. In fact, on many occasions since, he visualised what the woman was doing in the building which caused him to hang his head in pity.

The prostitute on the other hand would see the priest meditating and thought, *"What a good man. He sits and meditates daily and thinks about God. He always helps others in need. Ah well, I have to make a living."*

It happened that on the same day, the prostitute and priest died. They went to the gates of St Peter and asked to be admitted to heaven. Peter said to the prostitute, "you may enter," but denied access to the priest. The priest was upset. He scratched his head and pace then said, "You let this woman, who defiled her body daily to enter heaven but deny me, a servant of God?"

Peter replied, "This woman had five children to feed and a crippled husband to attend. She gave her life for her family so that they could live better and that her husband could receive the best medication. She had no education. She had no skills so she did what she thought she had to do."

The priest lowered his head as St Peter continued, "you on the other hand had everything given to you. Your parishioners gave you food and supported your monastery. Yes, you gave them support when it was needed but you also passed judgement on others. You used to lust over the prostitute, thinking about the activities going on behind closed doors, then you would pity her without knowing her circumstances and pray to God for her forgiveness."

The priest turned, ashamed of what he had heard and walked away.

Judging others, not trying to find out the nature of another persons problem or situation.

The birds and the orchid.

There was a man who owned a hobby farm where he and his wife grew plums in a small orchid. He and his wife used to sit at the end of the day and watch the birds swoop and take fruit from the trees. They enjoyed this activity and loved the birds. However, all good things must end, the man died and his wife sells the farm.

The new owner, a bachelor, also love the birds but he did not like them swooping to take the fruit. He thought about it then decided to build a big aviary around the orchid to keep the birds in. The aviary was electrified so that if the birds soared to swoop on the fruit, they would be electrified.

The birds soon learned that pain was associated with this so they took to eating the fruit which fell to the ground. This pleased the man since they kept the orchid clean and he still had his precious fruit on the tree. As new generations of birds grew in the orchid, they soon forgot how to fly.

Time passed and soon the bachelor grew tired of the farm and sold it.

The new owners, a young couple with two children were disgusted with the idea of trapping the birds so they pulled the aviary down to free the birds. They stood back to watch the birds fly off but nothing happened. The birds just continued to peck at the fallen fruit and none attempted to fly.

"Look! They have pulled the aviary down." A young bird said.

"It's a trick. If you fly, the strange force will hurt you and you will fall to the ground. Remember what the older birds have said." Another bird replied in caution. All the birds remembered and they refused to fly.

A friend of the new owners visited and was told of the plight of the birds. "I will bring one of my own birds. When they see it fly, these birds will copy and the problem will be solved." The friend told the owners.

The friend returned with his bird and put it with the others who regarded it with suspicion. The bird took off and soared into the sky and swooped down to the trees to eat the fruit on the branches. The other birds looked but did not fly. "It's a trick. This is a foreign bird and the work of the devil. If you try to fly, you will be hurt," an older bird said so the birds continued to scrounge for food amongst the fallen fruit.

Other birds soon flew into the orchid but still, the original trapped birds were reluctant to fly.

Fear of failure; lack of trust; lack of will to try; tied by a popular belief.

Meet Jim.

Jim was a happy teenager who was liked by everyone. He never spoke ill of any one and was always willing to help where he could.

His teachers at school loved him and he was never punished. Jim would put his hand up to ask or answer questions and often joked in class to make light of a difficult situation. He was never rude to his teachers and would often talk with a teacher at recess. Other students turned to him for help in class which he gave freely. Jim always handed his work in on time and gave no cause for concern.

Such was Jim's life. His friends out of school looked forward to his company and his parents loved him dearly. However, at home, he was limited in what he was allowed to do. For instance, his mother forbade him from making tea or cooking toast. "leave it to me," she would say. Jim's father would never allow him to use the mower. "Go and play," he would tell him.

Stop here think about Jim's plight so far, particularly about what his parents are doing.

The story continues,

Jim suffered from cerebral palsy which caused his muscles to twitch. Walking was slow for Jim and his hands would shake. One day, he almost pulled the mower on top of himself, and on another occasion, scolded his hand with hot water.

Do you hold to the same opinions as when I asked you to stop?

There is a need to have the full set of information before a value judgement can be made. When learning, listen so that all of the information is heard and no essential component is missing.

The axe. (Adapted from an old Chinese story)

There is a man who lives in an ordinary suburb who keeps an open fire in his house to create warmth in the winter. He purchases his wood in bulk, cutting it on demand rather than stock piling pre-cut wood. He had abandoned his old wood box. One cold day, he went to cut sufficient wood to ensure his comfort till the next morning. He went to the shed to get his axe but could not find it. He pondered over this, but could not think of any other place where he may have left the axe.

While in the yard, he saw the boy next door looking at him from over the fence. Everything about the boy said "I have your axe," but the man did not react, electing instead to get angry about his missing axe. "Hello" said the boy to the man, even the hello told the man that the boy took the axe. The boy smiled and this too said to the man, "I took the axe."

The man decided to purchase a new axe, rather than confront the neighbours about his suspicions. While backing his car out of the driveway, he saw the boy on the footpath, sitting on his bicycle watching. Again, everything about the boy indicated that he took the axe. On backing the car out, the man narrowly missed the boy and smiled to himself thinking, "serves you right you little thief."

On returning home, the man took his new axe and went to cut wood for the fire. He decided to cut more than necessary and went to store the excess wood in the old wood box by the house. In side the box was his old axe. He remembered that he put it in the box for safe keeping since his own children always went into the shed.

He saw the boy next door through a crack in the fence, nothing about him said, "I took your axe."

Judging others; not having all information; poor rationalising

Alice in Wonderland (Lewis Carroll)

Alice was walking along a path in Wonderland when she came to a fork in the road. "Oh dear, which path should I take?" She thought to herself.

She looked up into a tree and saw a Cheshire cat. "Please Mr Cat, can you tell me which path I should take?" She said to the grinning Cheshire cat.

"It depends on where it is you want to go," the cat said, smiling at Alice.

"Oh! I don't know really," she replied.

To which the cat said, "Then it doesn't matter which path you take."

Direction for studying; career path choices; Know how to reach your goal.

The frogs in a pond.

A group of tadpoles grew up together in a large pond. As frogs, there was always plenty to eat and a lot to do. There were logs a plenty and reeds to hide and play in. Even the land was safe as they leap-frogged all over the place.

One frog in particular didn't like to play with the other frogs and kept to himself. He stayed in the reeds or sat on a log, eating, until he became a large, fat frog.

"Why don't you come and play with us," the other frogs would say. "We know things about this pond that you don't and we could teach you."

"No thanks," the big fat frog would say as he munched away on a cricket.

The population of the wild life in the area increased as time went by, since the pond was full of water and food. Again, the frogs asked the fat frog to come with them, they had something to show him. Again, he answered, "No."

One day, a large bird flew into the pond and stood at the waters edge. The frogs went immediately into the reeds to hide, except the big fat frog. The bird flew over to a log and perched next to the fat frog, "I am looking for some supper, can I have anything that I want?"

"Suit yourself. There is plenty for everyone," the fat frog said.

The bird without any hesitation opened his mouth and ate the fat frog, "Ah, a very good meal indeed," he said as he flew off.

The other frogs came out of the reeds and lamented, "If he had only listened to us, he would have learnt what we were trying to tell him. Alas, he just wanted to do nothing and suffered the ultimate consequence."

(Listen to others, they may have a valid opinion: Learning takes place when action occurs.

Frogs

Two frogs where happily playing 'leap frog' when they came across a butter churn. "What is that?" One frog asked the other. "I don't know, lets go have a look," the other replied.

They hopped around the butter churn till they came across a stool. They leapt onto the stool then into the churn which was filled with milk. "This is a strange liquid," said one frog to the other. "It doesn't seem to be harming us, let's swim around for a while," the other replied.

The two frogs swam and swam until they began to tire. "Let's stop and rest for a while," said one frog to the other. Yes let's, but there is no where to sit," the other replied.

They tried to climb the walls which were too steep and soon the frogs were getting very weary. "I can't take much more of this. I am losing my strength," said one frog to the other. "Hang on. Don't give up. Something will happen just wait and see," the other replied.

"It's no use. I can't do it. Save yourself." And the frog fell slowly to the bottom of the churn.

The remaining frog cried out for its friend. It swam faster and faster around the churn then he noticed that the strange liquid was getting thicker. Before long, he could walk on top of the liquid and found that he could easily hop out.

If only his friend had tried that little bit harder, he too would have succeeded.

Never give up. Keep trying and a solution will be presented to you.

Woman on the Hill.

A woman was standing on top of a hill. Three villagers at the bottom of the hill were speculating as to why she was standing there. One man suggested that she was standing there because it was high ground and she was looking for a lost child. Another suggested that she was merely looking after her sheep which were grazing below. The third man suggested that she may simply be enjoying the warmth from the sun.

The three men climbed the hill to ask the woman why she was standing there. Each asked her in turn, suggesting their own reason for her being there. Each time she said 'no.' Finally one of the men asked, "Then why are you standing here?"

The woman replied, "Oh! I'm just standing.

A given situation can have many views attached to its meaning. The truth can only be revealed by listening from the beginning or asking. Sometimes doing nothing is its own reward.

Bow and Arrow.

A young boy used to love playing 'cowboys and Indians.' In particular, he used to enjoy playing the part of an Indian since he had a toy bow and arrow set where the arrows had rubber suction caps. When he grew to become a teenager, he saw a martial artist with a long bow. He longed to learn this art so he approached the bow master and asked if he would teach him how to draw the long bow. He was accepted.

The boy was a dedicated student. He attended the masters training venue regularly but he was given trivial jobs such as cleaning the great hall. "When am I going to handle a bow?" He asked the master.

"Time is your master my lad. When you learn patience I will give you a bow," the master replied. At last the master gave the boy a bow and taught him how to stand correctly while holding the bow. The boy held the bow for a year without any arrows and soon became impatient.

"When am I going to put an arrow in the bow?" He asked the bow master.

"When you can hold the bow correctly and show no signs of weakening," the master replied.

The boy practiced for another six months, perfecting his stance and grip on the bow. His arms strengthened and his stance was firm.

"Ah! You are ready to draw the bow with an arrow. Let me show you how," said the master who taught the boy how to insert the arrow and to draw the bow.

Learning requires patience and often the learning of small parts to gain greater understanding. Listening to advice rather than jumping in to do something that requires skill. Practice what has been taught to enhance learning.

The Zen Master

A Zen master was talking with a young monk who was trying to discover the path to enlightenment. The monk sat and told the master how he had tried everything and had thought about everything the master had told him, going beyond what he was told.

"I am confused." The monk reported to the master. "I listen hard and think constantly about reaching enlightenment but to no avail."

The master sat and listened, occasionally offering advice that was quickly absorbed by the monk who continued to tell the master of his beliefs.

"Will you join me in a cup of tea?" The master asked of his student.

The young monk was honoured and thanked the master who proceeded to pour out a cup of tea, filling it to overflowing.

"Stop master. You are over filling the cup." Said the young monk with concern.

"And so must you stop filling your mind with self grandiose ideas. Study what you have been taught and listen attentively to what is being said." The master said no more and the monk left with more insight than before the meeting.

Self grandiose ideas, not willing to listen, not paying attention to what is important, a need to give up some old beliefs.

Warm fuzzies.

There was once a small town where every individual appeared happy and were concerned for each other. They were used to giving each other *warm fuzzies* which meant that they listened to one another and offered advice and showed concern. They would help each other in times of need and ensured that no member of their community ever went without food, education and support. It was a happy community and everyone smiled to one another as they passed each other during the day.

Life was indeed good to the people and many who passed through the town, wondered at the serenity they experienced. Businesses boomed and local government was supportive of new initiatives.

The time came one day, when it was necessary to elect a new mayor since the current mayor was old but much loved. Elections were held and a new mayor was appointed. He was a new man to the town and desired to make change. "Why do you freely give away warm fuzzies?" He asked individuals he could trust. "Why not sell them after all, you worked hard for them." He introduced *cold pricklies* where everyone was expected to look after their own interests and ensure their own success, leaving others to them selves. No longer did people smile at each other on the street. No longer did neighbours help each other or offer suggestions. Expertise was hired out and would only listen to another for a cost or if it benefited them.

The success of many businesses failed and education became a drudgery rather than being an experience to enjoy and a mechanism for attaining success. People avoided the town and those who passed through no longer looked upon it in awe.

Time passed and elections were again due. A new mayor was elected. She was a woman who left the town many years ago and she had often dreamed of coming home. She also desired change and called a public meeting to introduce her ideas.

"I remember this town when we were giving away warm fuzzies. It was a happy place. Everyone helped each other and listened to the opinion of others. Schools were a place of wonderment where students were encouraged to seek success and teachers and students alike were interested in each other's progress." The mayor stopped to see the peoples reaction.

"Why should we give away our love and support so freely." One man called from the crowd. "I don't trust my neighbour and my kids hate school."

The mayor replied, "When I lived in this town those many years ago, businesses boomed. Look at business now. It has declined and is now governed by fewer people." She stopped to reflect then continued, "When I left, I took the ideas I had learned from this town and introduced them to other towns. They too prospered and everyone was happy. They gave up cold pricklies and started to give warm fuzzies to whoever came into their town. People were welcomed and everyone listened to each other and offered advice."

The town accepted the change. The retired mayor and those who could not change, moved away and continued to live their lives suspicious of others. It was indeed a happy place to be again.

Change; listening; happiness; values; concern

The football team.

A local district, senior football club had a player who consistently played poorly, but was allowed to play each week, if only for a short period because of his dedication.

The captain of the team complained to the coach one day after losing a game, because the unfortunate player fumbled the ball which allowed the opposition to score. "Either he goes or I go." The captain said to the coach.

The coach thought about it for a short time then approached the unfortunate player about his performance and suggested to him that the game of football was not for him and he may benefit by looking for another sport.

The unfortunate player left the team and was replaced by a fast young player who held the nickname of "hungry." Hungry always went for the ball. "Pass it to me," he would shout. Given a chance in front of goal, hungry would score. Others in his team would call for the ball when he held it, but hungry would never give it up. The other team members became disgruntled and soon, the team was losing more games than they were winning.

The coach reflected on the clubs history. In the past four years, the team had played in the finals, winning one grand final. Since hungry joined the team and the unfortunate player had left, the mood of the club was different and the team did not make the finals.

The unfortunate player was a team player, the coach remembered. He would do anything for the team, in fact, he was willing to sit on the side line for the good of the team. The coach used him as a runner to pass on game play, and he would motivate the players while passing on the coaches instructions. He never missed training and would ensure that he spoke to everyone of the players during the break in play to provide inspiration and to keep the players hope up.

Hungry on the other hand believed that he was bought into the team because he was the best player and the team could not win without him. He would steal the ball from his own players and blame them if the game plan failed.

Team work. Effort and concern for each other.

The Caterpillars

There is a species of caterpillar that follow a leader wherever it may go. They join in a procession, 'head to tail' and all move endless along the same path which is decided upon by the leading caterpillar.

One day, while in procession, the leader crawled up onto a metal lid and proceeded to walk around the rim. The other caterpillars followed until they were all on the lid, the leader meeting up with the last caterpillar in the procession. The circle was now unbroken and the leader could not be determined and none of the caterpillars broke away from the endless procession. They walked for days in a circle until eventually; they began to fall off the lid due to starvation.

Leadership. Following someone without question. Doing the same thing as everyone else. No thought for one's self.

The small girl

A young girl stood on the side of a pool, bent at the knees, arms backwards and rocking on her feet, trying to get the courage to jump into the water. Her father who was in the pool had his arms up ready to catch her. He was shouting, "come on darling, daddy will catch you." The little girl thought about it for a short time, still rocking on her feet then she launched herself into her father's arms. She took the plunge and jumped.

A teachers explanation:

Education can be like this. We are asking you trust us as we lead you toward the success you truly deserve. We are also asking that you take risks, daring to do what you might have thought unattainable. Jump into your education and put your trust in the staff, your parents and yourself.

Quotes

You are not bound by the things perceived, you are bound by the clinging. (Tilopa)

A teacher's explanation

If you hold the idea that you are a poor student in any subject for any reason, then you are doomed to remain poor in that subject. While you hold onto an idea, that very belief will drive your actions. A concerned parent may try to redirect your thinking but in the end, while you hold onto your original belief, if you fail to improve you will be able to say to your parents or teachers, "I told you so."

The self-fulfilling prophecy is driven by the idea that "I am right." If you want success, change what you think about that part of your life where success is required. You are capable, never let anyone say otherwise; not even yourself.

Great spirits have always encountered violent opposition from mediocre minds. (Albert Einstein)

A teachers explanation.

When it comes to academic achievement, we are sometimes *"damned if you do and damned if you don't."* Peer pressure can sometimes work to ensure that your work is completed to an average level while staff and parents will insist that you put in more effort! We do not need to be mediocre, just our self.

A student should not take to heart what others may say. If a student is achieving greatness at school, let us celebrate this greatness.

Aim at the sun and you may not reach it; but your arrow will fly far higher than if you aimed at an object on a level with yourself. (Judy Hawkes).

Guess who's interpretation.

Setting goals for one's self is very important, even more so if one aspires to greatness. You might aim to be the president of a company and reach junior executive level. Isn't this better than not aiming so high in the first place? Do those who sit and wait reach executive status?

You might want to complete a course at university. Do you wait to see if you get a "good enough" score, or do you work to ensure that you maximise your chances by aiming for a good score?

The mill cannot grind with the water that is past. (Herbert)

Yes, you guessed it.

An old proverb which, when taken literally, means that a mill used to grind wheat cannot make use of the water that has already passed the mills paddle wheel which is the source of power.

What about yourself? Has opportunity *already passed* you? If you can see **now**, something that can help you in the future, make use of that thing (or person) now, because once the opportunity passes, it will be too late. Put another way, *"make hay while the sun shines."*

Opportunity does not wait for anybody, it's like time. If the opportunity exists then make use of it, now.

There is a mountain: *"First there is a mountain, then there is no mountain then there is."* Profound words sung by Donovan in the 60's.

Me again.

There are probably many interpretations of these words, they don't matter much, what is important is that the students think about them and attach their own meaning. Progress can only occur if we are challenged. We may see obstacles from time to time, but we usually overcome them.

Only the mediocre are always at their best.

If we never try, we will never know our true potential and will go about our work doing what we always have done. We will never know that we can do better if we accept what is going on around us. Don't step back, leap forward.

Successful people gain success by going beyond their perceived limits. It is far easier to go about our daily lives without change, accepting what is, than to make an attempt to improve our life style and job chances.

Is your best good enough? Go beyond mediocrity.

Dripping water, in time, will cut a hole through stone.

When an individual has determination, s/he can achieve anything.

If one gives up on an activity then there are no gains. **Persistence** produces results, giving up leads to doubt in one's own ability.

One of God's greatest gifts is the ability to think. (unknown)

Love and thought are God's gifts and without thought, where would we be? Thought enables us to develop our individuality and our potential to achieve.

Idle thought however develops laziness and may possibly lead to poor social and work skills. We have an obligation to ourselves and to God to develop our life to maximise our use of thought.

One of the seven deadly sins, sloth, is the ability to use thought to get others to do what we should be doing ourself. Sloth "uses" people and develops a person of poor character. In work, school or play, we should ensure that we are thinking for ourself to solve problems that may arise during the day and indeed, our life.

Without thought, life is a happening.

If you build no castles in the air, you build no castles anywhere. (Attributed to Edison)

Ideas originate in the mind but, if that is where they stay then the idea will remain just that; an idea.

This is true of any action conceived in the mind. A student who knows that they must be completing homework, but who just thinks about it will probably succeed in raising their stress level about completing the action but leave the task incomplete. The same is true of adults.

For an *idea* to come to fruition, for a task to be completed, *action* must follow.

Did you know: students who day dream are less likely to complete homework than students who remain task focussed?

The greatest hazard in life is to risk nothing. The man, the woman who risks nothing, does nothing, is nothing. (Net results)

Risk taking is how businesses progress. Risk takers also climb the business ladder by making calculated risks. Unless we take risks, we may never know our true potential. Many businesses have closed because they did not take risks. They did not monitor the future.

Students too need to take risks. Unless a student risks making a mistake or dares to try something different, they may never know what they are capable of performing. *"To try at all is to risk failure."* It is better to have tried and failed than never to have tried at all. How else can we determine our potential? How else can we go the whole distance if we never take risks?

Newman cast a despairing glance at his store of fuel, but not having the courage to say no, a word which in all his life he could never say at the right time, either to himself or anyone else, gave way to the proposed arrangement......

(Charles Dickens)

Indecision, can't say no, procrastination, tardiness all lead to one thing, non-completion of a desired or required task.

By being indecisive, we also put emotional pressure on ourselves, which often leads to self doubt and a poor self concept. Is it worth it?

The turtle only makes progress when his neck is stuck out. (Rollo May)

Once an activity becomes habit, thinking becomes more rigid and consequently, to change ones attitude towards that activity will be fraught with difficulty. For example, if I believe that I am weak in maths and have constantly experienced this weakness, it is unlikely that I will improve unless I *"stick my head out"* and do something that changes how I behave in that subject.

We can all change, we need to take more risks and be more positive.

Luke Skywalker tried to retrieve his space craft from a swamp by using the 'force'. He did not succeed.

Yoda, a Jedi knight, insisted that he continue but Luke insisted, *"I can't do it,"* to which Yoda replied, *"that's because you do not believe."* (Star wars; Lucas)

We may not be a Jedi knight but how many of us say "I can't do this," to tasks that are being done by others. Often, what we think we can't do is a response to our previous experience of failure at that task. Persistence and perseverance will ensure that we indeed gain success at set tasks.

Don't give in. Persist. Ask for assistance if necessary.

The seed of mystery lies in muddy water. How can I perceive this mystery?

Water becomes clear through stillness. How can I become still?

By flowing with the stream. (Lao-tze)

We live in turbulent times. We each have a cross to bear, and often carry the cross all our lives when in fact, there was no need. Students go through their own personal trauma, sometimes exaggerating the cause by keeping the water muddy.

If we stir the mud in our lives, how can we ever effect change? If we allow the water to settle, the mud will clear and we will see a solution, or that the situation was nowhere near as bad as was originally thought! Sometimes, we need to flow with the stream of life before we can induce change. Resistance will stir the water and we will battle against the flow.

Sometimes as parents, we stir the water around our children by demanding perfection. How many of parents have insisted on A's from their children? If the child is struggling to meet a parents needs, when will they meet their own? Allow the child to grow and flow with the stream. When a child can see how they can improve in their own time, they will make the necessary changes.

Let's not stir the water. Flow with the stream and make observations along the way. Take time to sit and listen to your inner most thoughts. Don't dwell on the negative, relax and let a solution to your problem evolve.

What is firmly established cannot be uprooted. What is firmly grasped, cannot slip away. (Lao Tsu)

If you develop the habit of studying, you will not encounter difficulty when the need for study is increased, or if you need to study for a new topic. Whatever is practiced regularly, soon becomes second nature and less difficult to master.

Consistent study behaviour will improve your chance for understanding what might otherwise be a difficult concept. Once you learn a new concept, it will stay with you and may even help future learning, particularly if the concepts are related. Learning becomes easy if you keep up with your studies and master new concepts.

The difference between good and bad grades is often due to study habits. Poor habits may lead to poor grades and the concepts meant to be understood, soon slip away.

If you think you can't, you're right. If you think you can, you're right. (Ken Hatton)

We are responsible for our actions and inactions.

If I think that I can't achieve success then you can bet that success will not follow.

If I believe that I can achieve success, even if I need to learn something else first, then success is sure to follow.

Don't idle away the time in dreams of what could be. Go out and achieve your life's goals.

All difficult things of the world are sure to arise from a previous state in which they are easy, and all great things from one in which they were small. (Leo Tze)

How easy is it to let a situation get away from us, or to allow a task to suddenly become the most important event confronting us?

How much easier is it, and less distressing, to begin the task while it is only in its initial stage, rather than having to confront it in its entirety when the due date for its completion is due?

Begin small. Take small incremental steps towards its completion and great things can happen. If it is homework, potential errors can be corrected because they will be picked up if you continually look over your work. There is no room for error when you apply "the night before" approach to studying.

If you have made mistakes... there is always another chance for you... you may have a fresh start any time you choose, for the thing we call failure is not the falling down, but the staying down. (Mary Pickford)

Failure is in the eyes of the beholder. If you think that you have failed, then for certain, you have failed- through your eyes.

To another person however, they may see your setback as a hic- cup, knowing that with a change to your approach to the problem, a solution will be forth coming.

If you fall down, get up. Think about how you could approach the problem differently; don't put your self through anguish because you believe that you have failed.

Think of failure as a set back and work around it. You are worth it!

If you are lying on the ground, you must use the ground to raise yourself. (Chin-Ning Chu)

Whether it is despair, fear or procrastination, or whatever, we must use the negative aspect to raise ourselves from what could be the lowest point in our life.

A student who is weak in a subject can only improve if he recognises the weakness and begins to learn from his mistakes; not accept the mistake as defining who he is.

If we stay on the ground, we will soon be run over or passed by. By getting up and facing our weak moments, we can only grow.

A pessimist is someone who looks at the land of milk and honey and sees only calories and cholesterol! (Healthworks)

The world is an open forum to all students. You can embrace it with all its faults and achieve great success by challenging and changing your views, or let the world dictate where they will go from here.

It is important that you develop an opinion about what goes on around you. It is equally important that you do not let life events dictate your future.

The world is not all doom and gloom. You can be a success in this world.

I have spent my days stringing and unstringing my instrument, while the song I came to sing remains unsung. (R Tagore)

Most of the time, what is really needed is for a task to be started. It doesn't need to be done to perfection, it simply needs to be started then it can be worked on.

A perfectionist often starts a task then redoes it. But in the redoing, it never gets completed. The perfect essay, the perfect song, the perfect anything are still waiting to be done but in the meantime, a lot of people are gaining a lot of joy from completing what is their own work, no matter how imperfect it might be.

Waiting for the right moment, the right person, the right idea can only bring pain and while you wait, others will snatch success from you.

Enjoy life, enjoy education. Stop worrying about what others might think or whether the task could have been done better and get on with it.

Nobody makes a greater mistake than he who spends his life trying to avoid them. (Anon)

A great deal of learning takes place when we try and fail.

If failure is accepted then the amount of learning is very little. If the failure is investigated then much power is gained.

Problem solving occurs when difficult tasks are dared to be solved. It is easy to give in to difficulty, it takes a strong character to face a problem head on to seek a solution or gain success.

Gaining a quality education can be like this. If an individual gives up and waits for the solution then that individual can expect a mediocre education. If the difficult task is faced head on, then your education will be rewarding and success will be beyond your original expectations.

To dream of the person you want to be is to waste the person you are. (Anon)

To dream and do nothing is to denigrate not only who you are, but what you can achieve.

To dream and make changes in your life to make the dream come true is to improve on who you are and to broaden your capacity to achieve in life.

You are not your dreams but what is expressed by your thoughts, words and deeds. Become the person that you visualise and achieve satisfaction and greatness in your in your life.

All that we are is the result of what we have thought….(*Buddha*). Blessed is the man who finds wisdom, the man who gains understanding, for he is more profitable than silver and yields better returns than gold. (*Proverbs*). By three methods may we learn wisdom: first by reflection, which is noblest; second by imitation, which is easiest; and third by experience, which is the bitterest. (*Confucius*).

Wisdom and knowledge is not restricted to a particular sect or group of people. Each, in their own way readily provide inspiration, which can be used by all of us in our life.

In the study of Zen, it is often said, *do one thing at a time*. How true. A cluttered, racing mind can achieve very little. Be present in the now and attend to what it is you need to do. Ah, there is wisdom throughout history; even your parents can be wise.

A valid lesson can be learnt from the most unlikely source if we leave our minds open and remain receptive to what is being said. Wisdom is not restricted to the favoured few but is available to us all, through experience.